GABRIEL COULDN'T STOP KISSING CLARA.

He couldn't stop stroking her.

He couldn't stop indulging in the sensations rippling across his torso.

Fuck. He'd never experienced anything like this. His body was strung so tight he felt like he might explode without even being inside her. It made no sense, and yet, for the first time in his existence, he chose not to look for the practical recourse.

Instead, he allowed himself to *feel.*

Hot.

So. Fucking. Hot.

He ripped the towel from Clara's body and swallowed her yelp of surprise. His fingers remained locked in her hair, holding her to him as he devoured her with his mouth.

Sex had never held any value to him. Yet he would die if he ended this now.

All his principles and past learnings flooded his mind, trying to yank him back to some semblance of sanity, but all he could see was Clara. Her naked breasts pushed up against him. The slender column of her throat, oozing blood from the wound he'd created. Her rapid breaths and plump lips.

He kissed her again, harder this time, dominating her with his tongue and groaning at the delicious sounds she made in response.

All his decades of living paled in comparison to this passion. This sensation. This violent need to fuck.

This was what he'd been missing during each previous encounter—this yearning that plummeted him to a new reality of being.

There was no logic here.

No reasoning.

No edicts.

Just lust.

Immortal Curse Series Order

Book One: Blood Laws
Book Two: Forbidden Bonds
Book Three: Blood Heart
Book Four: Blood Bonds
Book Five: Angel Bonds
Book Six: Blood Seeker
Book Seven: Wicked Bonds

Immortal Curse World Books

(Bonus Stories & Immortal Curse Fun)
Elder Bonds
Blood Burden
Blood Skye

Blood Burden

Immortal
Curse
World

USA TODAY BESTSELLING AUTHOR
Lexi C. Foss

Blood Burden

Copyright © 2020 Lexi C. Foss

Editing by: Outthink Editing, LLC

Proofreading by: Katie Schmahl, Jean Bachen, Julie Robertson, & Shelley Charlton

Cover Design: Amala Benny with Mayflower Studios

Cover Photography: CJC Photography

Cover Models: Keith Manecke II & Kristen Alyss

Published by: Ninja Newt Publishing, LLC

Digital Edition ISBN: 978-1-950694-94-5

Print Edition ISBN: 978-1-950694-95-2

To Jean, for all your support and love. Enjoy your Gabriel ;)

BLOOD BURDEN

IMMORTAL CURSE WORLD
NOVELLA

BLOOD BURDEN

Welcome to the Immortal Curse world, where angels and vampires live in secret… for now.

Gabriel is a warrior. A Seraphim. An immortal of astute power and authority. He's lived his life beneath a cloud of stoicism and practicality. Only to have his entire existence turned over on its head because of *her*.

Clara. The witch who enchanted him with her empathy—a vampiric talent wreaking havoc on his ability to focus.

He's hell-bent on righting the wrong, even if it means killing her to restore his mental sensibilities.

However, not all battles are fought physically. Some require heart.

Clara's no normal adversary.
And she's about to bring Gabriel to his knees.

Author's Note: This episodic novella is part of the Immortal Curse world and best enjoyed when read as a companion story to the Immortal Curse series. Begin the journey today with *Blood Laws*.

GLOSSARY

PRETERNATURAL BEINGS

Fledgling (noun): The child of a male Ichorian and a human female, who has not yet been reborn as a Hydraian; they do not typically possess supernatural or psychic gifts until their immortal rebirth.

Hydraian (noun): An immortal offspring of a male Ichorian and a human female, who possesses two supernatural or psychic gifts and does not require human blood to survive.

Ichorian (noun): An immortal being of unknown descent who possesses one supernatural or psychic gift and requires human blood to survive.

Immortal (noun): A general noun designating a being who does not age and is immune to natural human death.

Progeny (noun): The term Ichorians use to refer to those they created through their turning process.

Seraphim (noun): A being who belongs to the highest order of angelic hierarchy.

GLOSSARY

KEY TERMS

Arcadia: Notorious Ichorian club in New York City that also serves as the primary meeting location for the Ichorian government.

Blood Laws: A series of ordinances created by the Ichorian governing board in response to the Treaty of 1747.

Catastrophic Relief Foundation (CRF): A global humanitarian aid organization headquartered in New York City with a secret paramilitary unit designed to destroy rogue supernaturals.

Conclave: The Ichorian governing board.

Edict: A law or rule issued by the High Council of Seraph.

Elders: The original Hydraians who also serve as the Hydraian governing board.

Fated Line: Seraphim who can foresee the future.

High Council of Seraph: Seraphim governing board.

Nizari: Ancient Ichorian assassins who hunt and kill fledglings.

Nizari Poison: A green substance notorious for killing fledglings and preventing their rebirth.

Sentinel: A soldier in the CRF unit designed to slaughter rogue immortal beings.

Treaty of 1747: An armistice between Hydraians and Ichorians to cease fire and live in their designated areas. Those who opt to cross these boundaries do so at their own risk.

Psst… Can I tell you a secret?

Blood Seeker was supposed to be about Gabriel and Clara. But Sethios demanded more page time, and my muse was helpless to stop him. I always listen to the voices. And he wasn't wrong in this case.

However, it didn't surprise me at all that Gabriel kept piping up throughout *Blood Seeker*. Nor did it shock me when he said, "We're going to continue my story and explore what happened in that Hydraian cell, right?"

This world is just so incredibly vast in my mind. I can't even begin to say how many avenues I stroll down just to see what everyone is up to. It's been with me for over a decade, and these voices are my home.

So I thought, why not create an Immortal Curse world to write some of these events in? They're not exactly key plot points for the story to move forward, but they are important character development scenes that I really want to be able to share. They just don't "fit" into any of the main sequences.

Like how Ezekiel met Skye.

Or what the hell happened between Gabriel and Clara when he went to visit her in Hydria.

Blood Burden explores the latter. It takes place during the end of *Blood Seeker* and the beginning of *Wicked Bonds* and sort of bridges the gap between them. The entire focus is on Gabriel and Clara, making this very character-driven.

It's a sexy little novella.

You'll get to see a very different side of Gabriel and learn more about Clara.

And it sets up *Wicked Bonds*.

All points in *Blood Burden*'s favor.
All fun.
All approved by Gabriel (well, um, mostly, anyway).
;)

Happy Reading <3
—Lexi

AN INTRODUCTION

FROM GABRIEL

My sister is better at this than I am. So if you haven't read her story yet, maybe go back and start there. I think she called it *Blood Laws*—based on the Ichorian governmental bullshit Osiris created. He built all of it to mimic the High Council of Seraph.

And if you've not read any of this world, then you have no idea what all of that means.

Right then, let me start over.

Ichorians are vampires. They'll argue this point, but they need human blood to survive. Hence, vampires.

Osiris is an ancient Seraphim (otherwise known as angels) who was exiled from the Seraphim world for reasons that are currently being questioned. He responded to his exile by creating an army of resurrected humans that are now essentially immortal. Those beings are the Ichorians I mentioned above.

There are also Hydraians, which are created when a male Ichorian impregnates a female human.

The offspring is technically mortal, but when killed, the being reawakens as an immortal with dual abilities.

It's all about the bloodlines and power and a myriad of other details.

Anyway, here's my story in a nutshell: I'm a warrior Seraphim. It means I excel at strategy and killing things. However, my primary purpose of late has been keeping my half sister, Stas, safe and preparing her for the future.

Pretty standard shit, except Stas is completely ungrateful and hates me. It's entirely impractical and detracts from the mission at hand.

I did the best I could with the destinies we were given. Once Stas finishes growing into her wings, she'll understand.

Or maybe she won't.

That was the whole point of having humans raise her—to provide her with a lesson on humanity.

It's something our kind—Seraphim—lacks.

We're practical. We see emotions as a waste of time. We make decisions based on the Fates (angels who can see the future). It's why I was created, and same with Stas.

Except, lately, things suggest the Fates haven't been providing altruistic guidance to the High Council of Seraph. In fact, it seems they want the famous Seraphim council to be overthrown.

It's all still subjective and up in the air.

But a prophecy claimed Stas is going to become a powerful force unlike any this world has ever seen and "destroy us all." The Seraphim assumed that meant Osiris and his abominations. But as of late, it seems as though the prophecy actually meant all of angel kind.

It's confusing, I know.

That's why I said to start at the beginning.

But hey, if you're here and want to see my little side adventure, then feel free to turn the page. I have an Ichorian to hunt down. I sort of borrowed her empathetic ability in order to test my humanity, and it's not gone as planned. So I'm going to ask her to fix it. If that doesn't work, I'll kill the source —a.k.a. her.

I have one final word of warning before we begin: I'm in Hydria right now, which is an island littered with those Hydraians I mentioned. They're like the Ichorians but don't drink blood. They also have dual powers. And they're extremely emotional.

I'll do my best to avoid conversing with most of them.

The story will be more efficient that way.

Right then. Grab a feather and fly along with me. I expect it to get bloody around here.

PROLOGUE

CLARA

Innocent until proven guilty.

Isn't that the phrase?

It doesn't seem to apply to me. Yes, I admitted to my supposed sins out loud, but Osiris compelled me to do it. I thought for sure they wouldn't believe me, that they'd at least question my loyalty shift. Except that wasn't the case at all. They threw me into this cell to be tortured for information—information I don't have.

I shiver. Cold. So, so cold. And alone.

It hurts.

The betrayal, the pain of their easy acceptance, the realization that those I thought were my family never saw me that way at all.

I curl tighter into my ball, trying to disappear. My mind broadcasts a mantra of self-loathing, repeating the words Osiris put there for all to hear.

Balthazar seems to question the repetition of my thoughts. I wish he could hear the ones screaming beneath, begging them to *hear* me. But only the superficial fake ones seem to process. The words that paint me as guilty. Claiming I betrayed them. Telling them I did it because Issac didn't want me after I'd been created for him.

Does he believe that, too? Does he think I actually feel that way after everything we've been through?

We never wanted each other.

He knows that better than anyone else.

I want to ask to speak to him, but I can't. I'm locked in a cell with no way out, frozen in a corner beneath a wave of agony no one but me can feel.

Time passes.

Questions continue.

Always the same. Always angry. I've never seen Luc look at me this way, like he wants to kill me. I'm terrified. I want to cry. I can't.

They leave once more.

I curl into myself, longing to scream, but no sound passes through my lips. I'm a puppet, controlled by strings I can't see. However, I feel them. Wrapped around my thoughts, dictating for me. Moving my mouth and tongue, speaking for me.

My throat aches with thirst.

It's been too long since my last feed, but they're keeping me weak, punishing me for a crime I didn't commit.

I wait for someone to question the sanity of this

plight, to wonder why I would do such a thing, to state that something isn't right.

But the time never comes.

I hear them now in the hallway—Luc's angry tones and B's calming ones.

My heart breaks a little more, then stops completely as a male with white-blond hair materializes into my cell like some sort of god.

No, not a god. A Seraphim.

I can't see his wings, but he has an ethereal edge around him. Or maybe that's all the trembling. Heck, I can't even tell if he's real. Perhaps I've grown delirious from lack of sustenance.

A laugh threatens my chest, but the compulsion demolishes it, leaving me shaking instead. I weave a little, attempting to dislodge the pain.

Back and forth.
Back and forth.
Back and forth.

That feels a little better. Oh, but he's next to me now, and he's so warm!

"I need a sample of your blood," he says, his voice deep and soft and just a little gruff. I rather like it.

Until his words register.

Blood?

But the compulsion refuses to let me speak, the word lodged in my brain as he wields a knife toward my arm. I long to flinch, to react, but I can't. Osiris's spell holds me captive, forcing me to endure the torment of his blade and the slice down my forearm. I can't even look at it, my focus is on some point in the room, my mind rebelling against the needs of my body to react.

It's agony personified, destroying me from the inside out as I battle an invisible net that holds me hostage to another person's whims.

Tears tickle my eyes yet refuse to fall.

Inside, I'm dying. I'm shredded. I can't focus or breathe or do anything other than *sway*.

I hate this.

I hate them.

I hate Osiris.

I hate myself.

How did I find myself in this hell? Why me? I can't even remember how it happened, but I recognize the power. I know whom it belongs to. I just don't know how long it's been in my mind.

I'm innocent! I scream again, but no one hears me. *Help me!*

Warmth blankets my side as the knife-wielding male falls to his knees. He trembles violently, releasing all the pain I keep buried inside.

My heart beats a little lighter with the reprieve, his agony mirroring my own, his cheeks wet with the tears I long to shed.

Sweet bliss!

But none of it is real.

It's all a strange concoction of fate, twisting and turning and driving the blade deeper into my heart.

I want to cry like him. I want to shake like him. Yet I remain locked inside this cage of perpetual anguish, silent and alone.

His light green eyes meet mine, my sadness reflected in his beautiful irises. I long to be like him. To be able to voice my own emotions.

He narrows his gaze, then shakes his head as voices spill into the room around us. I ignore them, my focus on the handsome male writhing beside me. I pretend to be him, to use him as my outlet for all the turmoil threatening to rip me apart.

But rage from the Elders snaps my focus, specifically Luc's.

He wants me dead.

I feel his hatred.

It's a mask he wears to hide his own grief, a way he handles the painful loss he believes I helped to cause.

There's no point in correcting him.

He'll never believe me.

My shoulders fall, my insides screaming once more. I'm lost to them all, to myself, to this horrible reality.

"Help her," the angel says in that gruff tone. "*Fuck*. Make it stop!"

I blink at him. Is he an empath like me? Can he sense the truth?

My chest aches with the thought, my breathing picking up a fraction before that menacing compulsion weighs me down again.

No! I want to feel this hope! To dream!

Such a beautiful man.

My savior.

Please feel me. Please know.

He appears angry, his green irises swirling with turmoil. "She's in agony." His big hands curl into fists, his muscular arms flexing with the movement. "Fix. It." Two words, spoken through gritted teeth.

Two words I will forever remember.

Two words that promise to change everything.

Because I feel the others in the room contemplating now, the confusion radiating off Balthazar an indication that perhaps he will listen to this mighty angel.

My guardian angel.

He looks at me one last time, then disappears from the room, confirming he's a Seraphim.

And I'm left with my captors and a terrifying male Ichorian.

Oh, maybe I was wrong. Maybe I am going to die after all. He's studying me in a manner that leaves me uneasy, his green eyes the same shade as his father's.

This is Sethios, son of Osiris.

Known for his sadism. Cruelty. Wicked ways.

He's also Stas's father.

Stas… who died on the beach.

That's it, then. They've brought him here to deliver my final fate.

Perhaps the angel will return to guide me to the afterlife.

Perhaps he never existed at all.

I close my eyes, awaiting my fate, only to widen them as I feel the strings beginning to loosen around my mind and body.

He's undoing the compulsion.

"Has Astasiya seen Clara since you imprisoned her?" he asks.

"No, why?" Lucian replies.

"Because I think my father left her a present to unravel," Sethios says as more pressure is released from my spirit.

He knows what Osiris did to me, I realize, my heart beating so fast it threatens to break. *He knows… because the angel felt me. He saved me, my guardian, sweet angel… the empath who liberated… me.*

It feels so freeing, so gratifying, until the agony inside me is finally allowed an outlet through my mouth.

Causing me to scream.

And scream.

And scream.

Words I don't mean to say leave my lips, threats I had thought and couldn't voice, statements about family, betrayal—it all roars out of me. My fist meets Balthazar's jaw as he tries to touch me, my mind too caught up in the horror to focus on the present.

The only thing that remains positive inside me is

the connection to the angel. The male who felt me. The male who demanded they fix it.

I only wish I knew his name.

One day, I'll find him and thank him.

My savior with the light green eyes. *My angel.*

CHAPTER ONE

GABRIEL

GABRIEL'S SISTER was about to mist into a trap laid by one of the most dangerous Seraphim of all time.

Leela was busy helping a lab-created abomination give birth to a child.

Ezekiel was guarding a prophetess.

Vera was fuck knew where.

And Gabriel floated over the beach outside of the prisoner hut in Hydria.

He ran through the priorities in his head for the millionth time, wondering why he'd chosen to be here over all of the aforementioned places. His sister could probably use the backup, and Leela could probably use some assistance. Yet Gabriel chose his own fate over theirs.

After decades of always putting everyone else before himself, it felt a little strange to take a moment to satisfy his own curiosity. But he needed the witch locked up inside that hut to fix him.

She was the empath who had turned on his emotions. Now she would help him turn them off.

Or he'd kill her. Because Gabriel didn't have time for this sensation nonsense. He needed it to end. Now.

Technically, it'd been his idea to absorb her gift. It wasn't the first time he'd used his Seraphim abilities to do so—all he needed was a drop of the being's blood to inherit whatever talent he or she possessed.

However, this enchantress's abilities were haunting him. Even now he was tempted to take in the starry night sky and sigh.

Yeah, fucking *sigh*.

Which caused his lips to twitch down—something they never did before—in annoyance.

He shook off the feelings and forced a stoic expression. It served no practical purpose to approach this from an emotional point of view. He'd demand the female fix him, then go about his next task.

Or maybe he would nap.

He didn't sleep much these days, and he could feel the exhaustion weighing down his limbs.

Yes, a nap would be nice.

Nice?

He growled at the ridiculous sentiment and misted toward the hut on the beach, determined to squash this emotive nonsense.

Clara's cell was toward the back, beyond the two guards waiting in the hallway. Gabriel didn't stop to ask for permission, just misted on by them in his ethereal state. Since they were Hydraians, they couldn't see him. It was one of the many perks of being a Seraphim. His lack of emotions was usually one, too.

He nearly scowled again but managed to correct the motion of his face as he breezed on through the door into the white-walled room.

A memory of before nagged at him—of the poor blonde female huddled in a corner, shifting from side to side to some beat only she could hear.

She didn't sit there now.

He materialized into his corporeal state and spun around on the concrete floor toward the shower. She stood just inside, gaping at him.

Naked.

Fuck.

Why did this keep happening to him? First his mother decided to fly around without clothes on, and now this female stood soaking wet beneath a shower spray.

However, unlike the former, this sight somewhat intrigued him.

No. No, it doesn't intrigue me at all, he corrected himself. *Pleasures of the flesh are a mortal concept.*

He'd tried sex a few times and didn't understand what all the fuss was about. Aside from a minor physical reaction of relief, it did nothing for him.

Of course, none of those conquests looked like Clara, with her slender waist, long legs, and above-average breasts. He reckoned they would fit in his palms rather nicely.

Not that he was thinking about it. Because that would be impractical.

Gabriel cleared his throat. "I need your help fixing something," he told her.

She squeaked in response, causing him to frown. Which made him scowl. And then growl in annoyance at his uncooperative face.

"Do you see what you've done to me?" he demanded, pointing at his facial patterns. "I keep... *reacting*. I need you to fix it."

Clara yelped again, this time adding a jump to the sound that caused her towel and clothes to fall off their precarious perch on the cement ledge beside her to the ground below. Right into the water pouring down from the showerhead above.

"Perhaps the chair would have been a better place for that?" Gabriel suggested, pointing to said chair five feet to the left of the open shower.

She could also do with a shower curtain and a proper bed. Because the half-heartedly dressed mattress on the floor appeared lumpy and cold.

He supposed she deserved the fate since she'd betrayed her friends and family. Except, he wondered if that was true. She'd been in so much pain when he'd taken her blood. And not because of his knife. That sort of agony had been soul-deep and horrifying. It sent a chill down his spine now as he recalled the sensation.

Gabriel never wanted to experience anything like that again.

However, he had to ask: "Are you okay?" Because if she was still in pain, then he… well, he would have to do something.

Why? he wondered. *Why do I feel obligated to help this woman?*

Fuck, this was confusing.

All of it.

He despised these impractical inclinations. He just wanted his sanity back!

"You're… you're real," she breathed.

He blinked at her. "Uh, yes?"

"And standing in my cell."

He glanced down at his feet, his lips threatening to do that irritating thing again. "That is what this position is typically called, so yes."

Why was she asking him such asinine questions? Was she broken? Was that why he felt so strange from her blood? Had she somehow infected him with whatever this was?

"W-why?" she asked in a whisper. "Are you here to cut me again?"

"Did I hurt you?" he countered, wondering if that was the cause of her weirdness.

"No. You saved me. Now they know the truth."

His eyebrows wanted to lift, but he refused the action. "What truth?"

"That I'm not the mole."

Well, that was news to him, but he'd been a little

busy since he'd last seen her. "If you're not the mole, then why are you still in this cell?"

"To help them catch the culprit," she replied, wincing with the words. "I'm stuck here until they figure out what really happened."

"But you didn't betray them."

"No. I didn't."

"Yet you're still being punished."

She lifted a shoulder. "Where else would they send me?" She looked down at her soaking-wet towel and clothes, then blanched, her hands suddenly lifting to cover herself. "Oh my God, I'm naked."

"Clearly," he replied. "The water is running, too." Since they were stating obvious things, he figured he would mention that tidbit, as the shower was wasting resources with her not using it for the desired purpose.

"Turn around!" she snapped.

He glanced over his shoulder. "Why? There's nothing there."

"Because I'm naked!"

This time he let his eyebrows pull down because he couldn't help it. "Why would that require me to turn around?" If he was being honest, he much preferred not turning around. Which was a problem he'd have to evaluate later because he shouldn't like looking at her in this state. However, a pretty blush turned her pale complexion a delectable red shade that

14

seemed to reach every part of her exposed form.

Embarrassment, he realized. *Because I'm seeing her naked*.

Right.

She was originally born human, so this type of situation would bother her.

Hence the reason she wanted him to turn.

He sighed and did as she asked, when another thought popped into his head. "Are those your only clothes?"

"Yes," she said, that single word holding an emotion he couldn't define. So he glanced back to see the tears glistening in her eyes.

"Are you in pain again?" he asked, worried she would start doing that mute swaying thing she did when they first met.

She turned off the water and wrapped the sopping-wet towel around herself, her lower lip trembling. "I'm fine."

She didn't look all that fine. Beautiful, yes. But also very sad. She flicked a tear from her eye and cleared her throat.

"Why are you here?" The words came out a little hoarse, like she had to force them past the emotion in her throat.

"Hmm, I thought they fixed you." However, she didn't appear to be any better than the state he'd found her in before. Well, apart from the fact that she spoke now. That was an improvement.

Clara merely looked at him and attempted to tighten the towel around herself—a towel that wasn't doing anything other than causing more water to trail down her already wet form.

He glanced at her ruined clothes, then around the cell for anything she could use. The thin bedsheets might work, but that would leave her with a bare mattress for sleeping on later.

Something nagged at him, an irritating little gnat that left him uncomfortable. He couldn't seem to ignore it despite his practical inclinations to just disregard her conditions and move forward with the reason he'd dropped by.

"These accommodations aren't suitable for this." They needed to engage in an important conversation, and she was too miserable for that to happen.

Gabriel misted out of her cell to his flat in New York City. It was the one he kept hidden and stayed at when he needed to remain close to the Catastrophic Relief Foundation headquarters but didn't want anyone to find him. He had another apartment he kept for employment records and to appease his former boss. That property was no longer relevant, but this one suited a reasonable purpose. Especially now that his home in the South Pacific was compromised.

He glanced around, searching for anything suspect, and found it as clean and untouched as he'd left it weeks ago.

The red feathers at his back propelled him toward his master bathroom, where he selected a plush white towel. This would do much better than the one Clara had back in her cell.

With a nod, he returned to find her on the floor again, tears rolling down her cheeks as she sobbed into her wet clothes.

Fuck. She actually was broken after all.

He sighed—a sound that was truly starting to grate on his nerves—and held out the cotton fabric for her. "Here, this will—"

She shrieked—yet another sound he really didn't like—and covered her heart with her hand. "Stop doing that!" The words were sharp, but her expression lacked reprimand. Then her eyes dropped to the towel, and a fresh wave of tears began.

He cleared his throat, decidedly uncomfortable with the direction this entire conversation had gone. "I…" Yeah, he didn't know how to finish that statement, so he just held out the dry fabric for her.

She stared at him for a moment and sniffled. Then she pushed back up to her feet and traded her damp towel for the item in his hand. A shiver went through her as she swaddled herself in the plush cotton, her pupils dilating in response. It was a much nicer towel than the one on the floor, causing him to look again at her soaked clothes near the shower.

"You need better accommodations," he said.

Seraphim prisoners were at least provided sterile conditions. And if what she said earlier was true, then she shouldn't even be a prisoner. "Let's go."

"Go? Go where?" she asked, her voice catching at the end.

"My flat. I'll find you some dry clothes to go with that towel, then we can talk."

"Talk about what?"

"Emotions," he said flatly and held out his hand for her. "Misting will feel a little weird at first, but you'll get used to it."

"Misting?"

"To my flat," he finished for her. "Yes."

"I… I don't understand."

What wasn't there to understand? "I'm taking you to my flat in New York City so I can give you some new clothes and we can talk about your empathetic abilities." He uttered the words slowly, hoping they registered.

"What about Luc? He won't want me to leave."

Gabriel snorted and pulled out his phone to shoot a text to Ezekiel. *Tell the Hydraian King I've taken Clara. He can have her back later.* He hit Send and slid the phone back into his pocket. "It's handled." He held out his hand again. "Let's go."

"But I don't even know your name," she said. "I mean, I think I know who you are. But… we've not really met."

He blinked at her. *Formalities? Now? Really?* "Gabriel," he informed her. "Warrior Seraphim.

Former CRF Sentinel. Stas's half brother. Anything else?"

"I thought that's who you were," she replied softly. "Okay. And you're sure Luc will be all right with this?"

His pocket buzzed as she spoke. He didn't bother to look at the message, certain Ezekiel would cover this for him. "Yes. I'll return you as soon as we're done talking." *Alive or dead,* he added to himself. *Depending on how helpful you prove to be.* "Can we go now?"

CHAPTER TWO

CLARA

CLARA STARED at the strong hand before her. It looked so inviting and warm. As an empath, she craved touch. And it'd been so long since someone had held her. Well, aside from Balthazar. He'd tried to comfort her after everything that had happened, but she'd not wanted him or anyone else to touch her then.

But Gabriel was different.

He was her angel.

The one who'd saved her.

The male who had demanded they *help* her.

And now he wanted to take her to his apartment in New York City. It seemed a bit sudden, just like his appearance in her cell. Yet she found herself wanting to go with him. An odd inclination, considering she was half-naked and couldn't read his emotions.

But she felt safe with him. Perhaps because he'd saved her before. Or maybe it was the peppermint spice taunting her senses from the soft towel he'd given her. It lulled her into a strange sense of comfort, one that seduced her into pressing her palm to his.

The touch sent a jolt down her spine, the electricity humming between them and setting her blood on fire just as the world shifted into a blur.

Her stomach clenched at the foreign movement, her lips parting on a gasp.

Oh!

She wasn't sure she liked this at all. It was different from Jacque's usual teleportation. This felt... *wrong*. Like she was intruding on an ethereal network of power that she shouldn't have access to.

Her grip on Gabriel's hand tightened, and she pulled him closer to wrap her free arm around him to hold on, afraid he might lose her in this network of strange weblike sensation. His palm remained steady in hers, but he followed her lead and returned her embrace, his strong arm encircling her waist as they misted together as one.

She sighed against him, immediately at peace despite the turmoil rolling through her insides. Because this was what she craved. Just to be held. And his lack of emotions helped, too. She couldn't sense anything from him, granting her a peace unlike any she'd ever experienced.

It took her a moment to realize they'd arrived. However, she didn't let go, her body and mind needing just a few more minutes of this serenity.

He didn't speak or push her away, just kept his

arm around her, providing her with a protective hold that shielded her from everyone and everything else.

This was her savior. Her guardian angel. The man who had initiated her freedom from the persuasive chains that had held her prisoner for far too long.

Thank you, she wanted to tell him. *Thank you for seeing the truth when no one else did.*

But Clara didn't like words. She preferred action. Perhaps because of her innate empathy. She so often saw through the statements of others and to the underlying emotion beneath. So much manipulation, and false comments, existed in this world. But actions provided proof in a myriad of ways.

Which was why she went to her toes and pressed a kiss to his cheek. It served as a note of affection coupled with her gratitude. Only, his warm skin seduced her into lingering a little. He just smelled so good. And his masculine heat, oh, she wanted to wrap herself up in it and never let go.

All of her lovers were mortal because she required them for sustenance. While Aidan had often invited her into his nest, she rarely indulged him. It just didn't feel right because she could always sense the presence of his love for another.

Issac and Amelia's mother.

He never spoke of her, not around Anya or Nadia, but Clara had always known of his preference for the woman he'd lost three centuries ago. That wasn't to say he didn't love the women he'd turned into Ichorians—he did—but he mourned his loss, too. And that always left Clara feeling a bit uncomfortable when joining her maker and his harem in the bedroom.

So she indulged her need for touch in temporary ways with human males, using them primarily for blood and also for sex.

Gabriel was… different.

A Seraphim.

An immortal who could potentially dominate her and not the other way around.

Clara lived in a constant state of having to coach her lovers on how to please her, the majority of her mortals too inexperienced or gentle to really give her what she needed.

That wouldn't be a problem with Gabriel.

Her thighs clenched with the possibility.

Then her mind caught up and reminded her that he'd brought her here to talk, not to indulge in sensation and touch.

Except he hadn't let her go.

Actually, he held her rather tightly, if a bit stiffly. Was he even breathing?

Her lips were still against his cheek. She could feel his flexed jaw, his tension palpable. But was it the good kind or the bad kind? She couldn't read his emotions to be able to tell, so she flattened her feet on the wood beneath her soles and shifted back just enough to read his light green eyes instead. Only, they were masked with indifference.

She swallowed at the sight, uncomfortable by his clear disinterest. "I... I just wanted to thank you." Her words came out breathy.

"For?" he prompted, his eyebrow inching upward, only to straighten half a beat later. An odd reaction, almost like he'd tried to stop himself mid-movement.

"Saving me," she whispered.

"I didn't save you. I'm borrowing you. Once we're done talking, I'll return you to your cell." His arm flexed along her lower back with the statement, the action contradicting his term. It felt as though he didn't want to return her at all, but continue to hold her.

How interesting.

From what Aidan and Luc had said, Seraphim didn't feel. They were stoic beings who preferred reason over emotion. Gabriel appeared to be struggling with that concept. Was that why he needed to talk to her about empathy? Did he need to understand how to feel?

She could teach him that.

So long as he agreed to continue holding her like this. Because, sigh, he felt amazing. Like home. Incredibly warm. Masculine. Strong. *Safe*.

Clara gave in to the urge to nuzzle his chest, which stirred a choked sound from him. His arm turned to granite against her lower back, his hand squeezing hers. Not painfully. But… possessively.

She looked at him again, this time catching the flare of his nostrils. "What are you doing?" he asked, his voice strained.

"Indulging in touch."

"Why?"

"Because I prefer it over words."

"Why?" he repeated.

"Words lie. Actions don't."

He stared at her. "Actions can contain lies. I once led Stas to an exam at the CRF that I knew would hurt her, just to maintain my cover. But that doesn't mean I wanted to bring her to harm. However, I did know she'd survive it since she's a Seraphim."

It was the most he'd said to her thus far, and she found herself fascinated by the deep tenor of his voice. Clara was also intrigued by the hint of regret in his gaze. She wondered if he even realized he'd just spoken that statement like he was confessing a sin he wanted to get off his chest.

"You can more easily detect untruths within an action," she replied slowly. "You can always tell which ones lack heart." She suspected the event he just described would have in some way displayed his discomfort with the act.

Or perhaps he'd hidden it well beneath his cloud of stoicism.

But his decision to continue holding her now

suggested he didn't have as much control over his emotions as he thought he did. He hadn't tried to push her away or release her but merely held on as though he didn't want to let her go.

She didn't mind.

He felt good against her.

"Lacking heart relates to emotions," he said after a beat of silence. "However, Seraphim do not feel. Everything they do is practical. Yet lately, I suspect many of their actions are founded in lies."

"Is that a confession or an observation?" she wondered out loud.

"I think it might be both." His lips curled down. "You're bewitching me again."

"Bewitching you?"

"Yes." He studied her for a long moment, his light green eyes giving nothing away. "I've been experiencing side effects from your empathy."

Now it was her turn to frown. "What do you mean?"

"When I imbibed your blood, I borrowed your ability. It was only meant to be temporary to test my emotional levels before meeting with the High Council of Seraph. However, it's left behind a few imperfections that I would like fixed."

Clara blinked at him. He'd mentioned needing a sample of her blood that day, but no one had told her why. They'd all been too consumed by the revelation of her innocence. Even she'd forgotten to ask. Part of her hadn't really cared because the result of his actions had freed her.

But now he'd provided her with a reason.

"What's the High Council of Seraph?" she asked. "And why did you need to test your emotional levels?"

His arms remained strong around her, yet his face continued to give nothing away. "The High Council of Seraph is the Seraphim governing body. To stand before them with any sign of emotion could result in a rehabilitation sentence, something I would prefer to avoid."

"Oh." She mouthed the sound, her mind processing the information. Tristan had told her about Gabriel's true nature, but she hadn't actually met him, or any other Seraphim, before. They could apparently go invisible and teleport. And borrow abilities by drinking blood.

That wasn't terrifying at all.

"Unfortunately, your empathy has left a lasting imprint," he continued, oblivious to her thoughts. "Which brings me back to the reason I misted into your cell—I need your help to remove the sensations lingering in my system."

"Um, maybe you should talk to B?" she suggested. "He can manipulate emotions. I just feel them." Although, she felt nothing from Gabriel now. Other than his hard body, of course. But emotionally, he was a blank page. Something she found rather soothing. It could be exhausting having everyone else's emotions mingling with her own.

"Balthazar's busy delivering Lizzie's baby," Gabriel replied. "I—"

"She's gone into labor?" Clara interjected. "Already?" Lizzie was only a few months pregnant. Maybe four at most. "Is she okay?"

"I'm sure she's fine." Gabriel's tone held a touch of impatience. "However, I'm not. So I need you to help me."

She considered him for a moment, noting the strain around his eyes. It hadn't been there a few seconds ago, but it appeared now, displaying a hint of desperation that she suspected this male didn't typically experience.

"What exactly are you feeling?" Maybe it wasn't related to her emotions at all, but something else entirely.

"I…" He clenched his jaw, his frustration palpable. "*Everything.*" His brow crinkled as he glanced down at her, then lower to their embrace. "We're hugging." His arms turned brittle around her. "*I don't hug.*"

He released her as though she burned him, and began pacing. "You've enchanted me," he accused. "This can't continue. You need to fix it." He stopped and spun to face her. "Tell me how to fix it."

She felt cold without his heat, the towel around her doing little to replace the natural warmth of his body. However, he wasn't here to comfort her. Instead, he needed her help. And as he'd saved her, she more or less owed him a favor in return. So it was a fair request.

Only, she had no idea where to start.

"Can you tell me what emotions you're experiencing?" she asked. "Perhaps we can start there and work backward so you can… remove the emotion?" This was probably one of those moments where she shouldn't voice her thoughts out loud, but rather consider them first. Because that one came out sounding utterly ridiculous.

How does one remove an emotion? Yeah, well done, Clara, she chastised herself.

Except Gabriel seemed to be considering her idea. "You're saying I need to identify the emotion to block it," he said slowly.

"Uh, well, yes, but—"

"Which means I need to better understand the feelings to know what they mean," he continued, not hearing her. Or perhaps just ignoring her.

"Um, that could help," she started, uncertain of how to finish the statement.

"Because then I would know what the sensations are tied to and be able to cut it off at the source." He nodded, his pacing resuming. "Yes. This could work. But I would need to know more about what I'm feeling in order to identify them."

"I can't sense anything from you," she said softly. "So I don't know how to help with that part."

"Your empathy will work on me if I drink from you again," he replied, stopping before her once more. "I need more of your blood. Then you can help me understand what I'm feeling, which will allow me to destroy the source." A blade seemed to materialize in his hand, causing her to jump backward.

"Whoa. Hold on."

"I'm just going to slice your forearm like I did last time." He advanced on her.

She skipped to the side and threw up a palm to stop him. "Gabriel. Stop."

He halted midstep, his brow coming down. "I don't understand. This was your idea. Did I misinterpret it?"

Her idea? She'd asked him to describe his feelings, not cut her arm. He was the one who came to this conclusion. Sure, the plan had merit, but... "I need a minute to process the, uh, knife." *And pretty much everything else*, she added to herself.

It was a lot for her to accept. All she'd wanted to do was take a shower to wash away the grime of the cell, and then he'd appeared like some angel of the night, only to whisk her away to New York City. Now she stood before him in a towel, and he wanted to cut her.

She eyed the knife and swallowed.

"That's such a cold way to drink blood," she whispered, more to herself than to him.

"It's practical."

"Is it?" She shivered at the thought of his steel edge against her skin. "You only took a few drops last time."

"That's all I need."

"So more won't give you a strong dose of my power?" She wasn't sure how the Seraphim imbibing system worked, but she knew a deeper feed from a human sustained her Ichorian need for blood longer.

He studied her again, his contemplative silence intimidating yet welcome. She couldn't remember the last time someone had taken her so seriously. Everyone always saw her as soft and sweet but never regarded her as an intellectual. Mostly because she kept her thoughts to herself. Balthazar often overheard them; however, she didn't see him often, and when she did, he kept her confidence.

She'd always preferred that.

But with Gabriel, she rather liked that he paid attention to her and listened.

"You're right," he said finally. "Perhaps I should take more. Should I cut your wrist?"

Her eyes widened. "What? No!" That was absolutely not what she expected him to say. "Why can't you just bite me like, well, like an Ichorian would?"

"Biting is intimate."

"I'm an empath," she retorted. "Everything about me is intimate."

More silence.

More studying.

She swallowed, his intensity stirring goose bumps down her spine. His features were striking and outlined by the low light coming in through the floor-to-ceiling windows beside them.

Gabriel was exactly what an angel should look like, with his windswept blond strands—one of which kept falling into his eye—his defined cheekbones, and his chiseled jawline.

Everything about his face was symmetrical and flawless, almost eerily so. Yet it also made him breathtakingly handsome, marking him as the kind of male who would warrant second looks upon entry into a bar.

Just like B and Luc.

Except Gabriel lacked their sexual prowess. Instead, he exuded indifference. Which probably caused a lot of girls to chase him, just to try to break through his impenetrable walls.

"Okay," he murmured, sliding the blade back into the pocket of his jeans. "Where do you want me to bite you?"

She gaped at him. "Seriously?"

"I don't joke," he replied flatly. "So yes. *Seriously*. I've never bitten anyone. But as it's your preference to the blade, I'll allow it. I need you to help me, so I'm expecting this to make you agreeable."

Such practical words.

But she caught the flare of his nostrils when he said he'd never bitten anyone. He was intrigued by the prospect of her being his first. Was it normal for a supposedly stoic Seraphim to feel curious?

She cleared her throat. "I, uh, I would prefer my neck." It would allow her to feel his body against hers again and borrow a little more of that strength. She'd gone too long without touch, leaving her bereft and cold.

That was the downside to her ability—she spent so much time surrounded by emotion that she didn't know how to handle it when it all disappeared. She also constantly craved the warmth of another, longing just to be held and surrounded by love.

Gabriel wouldn't provide her with that, but he could at least be warm for her.

"The artery there will give me what I need," he said. "I accept that location."

His serious tone almost made her smile, only he was already advancing on her again. He grabbed her hip this time to stop her from moving away, his opposite hand going to her hair as he threaded his fingers through her wet strands.

Such an intimate hold.

His clean scent overwhelmed her nostrils, delighting her senses.

Then he bent his head toward her neck. "I'm sorry if this hurts," he said, the words gruff against her skin. He sank his teeth into her vein, sending a jolt of pain down her spine, only to be followed by an ecstasy unlike any she'd ever experienced.

Fuck. This man was different from anyone she'd ever met.

No foreplay.

No warning.

Just action.

She dug her nails into his shirt, holding on as her knees threatened to buckle beneath the pleasure his embrace evoked from within her.

Pure.

Hot.

Bliss.

Oh God, she thought, shaking against him. *He's going to make me come from his mouth alone, and we're not even doing anything.*

Her thighs clenched, the heat blossoming inside her beginning to spiral out of control. She considered telling him to stop, but his hand left her hip as his arm encircled her back, pulling her closer.

Into his responding interest.

Shit. She could sense him now, his emotions whirling into an intense tornado that threatened to destroy them both if not tamed.

Only, his whirlwind of emotions heightened her own, driving her headfirst into the eye of his incoming storm, where together they exploded into an array of feelings that stole her breath.

Could he sense it? The lust pouring over them? Heating their blood? Dampening her thighs? Thickening his shaft?

She trembled, his name falling from her lips, her

mind lost to the sensations of their mounting arousal.

I should end this, she thought. *I should… I should run. I… I don't know how. Oh, oh, sweet…* She groaned as his hardness met her lower belly, his body providing the relief she'd gone without for too long.

"Gabriel…"

He shook against her, his teeth leaving her skin. "What is this?" he asked, his voice hoarse. "How have you bewitched me now?"

"Attraction," she managed to say, her tongue thick in her mouth. "Mutual… attraction."

No. That wasn't good enough. She'd felt mutual attraction before. This… this went well beyond that. This existed on an entirely new plane of existence. He'd inherited her power, thereby playing it back at her and ramping the emotions up between them to a dangerous crescendo of *need*.

Her knees gave out then, but his arm around her waist kept her upright, his grip in her hair tightening. "I've fucked before." His tone held an accusation. "But I've never experienced *this*."

She wasn't sure what exactly he meant but nodded anyway. Because she hadn't experienced this either.

"What are you doing to me?" he demanded, pressing his cock against her, seeking friction.

She moaned in response, the towel too abrasive against her skin.

He pulled away to look down at her, his pupils

blown wide with fury and desire and a horde of other emotions that just caused their tornado to spin faster. "Little witch," he accused, his eyes dropping to her mouth. "I... Tell me how to stop it."

She shook her head, unable to comply. Because she didn't know. She just *wanted*. "Kiss me," she begged. "Do something. Anything." She hadn't come from his bite but had been so, so close. She yearned for more, *anything* he would be willing to give. "Please, Gabriel. Please."

He glared at her, and for one split second, she sensed her impending death—his resolve palpable.

Only, it was gone in the next breath as his mouth captured hers, turning the spiral between them into an inferno. All it took was his tongue, and she lost herself to him entirely.

He owned her.

Utterly and completely.

So long as he never stopped touching her.

CHAPTER THREE

GABRIEL

Gabriel couldn't stop kissing Clara.

He couldn't stop stroking her.

He couldn't stop indulging in the sensations rippling across his torso.

Fuck.

He'd never experienced anything like this. His body was strung so tight he felt like he might explode without even being inside her. It made no sense, and yet, for the first time in his existence, he chose not to look for the practical recourse.

Instead, he allowed himself to *feel.*

Hot.

So. Fucking. Hot.

He ripped the towel from Clara's body and swallowed her yelp of surprise. His fingers remained locked in her hair, holding her to him as he devoured her with his mouth.

Sex had never held any value to him.

Yet he would die if he ended this now.

All his principles and past learnings flooded his

mind, trying to yank him back to some semblance of sanity, but all he could see was Clara. Her naked breasts pushed up against him. The slender column of her throat, oozing blood from the wound he'd created. Her rapid breaths and plump lips.

He kissed her again, harder this time, dominating her with his tongue and groaning at the delicious sounds she made in response.

All his decades of living paled in comparison to this passion. This sensation. This violent need to fuck.

This was what he'd been missing during each previous encounter—this yearning that plummeted him to a new reality of being.

There was no logic here.

No reasoning.

No edicts.

Just lust.

It spiraled all around him, consuming his every thought and action. His dick pulsed for it. His balls begged for it. His stomach clenched with it.

"Clara." Her name came out on a growl, his hand on her hip bruising as he tried to pull her closer. Only, she was already pressed up against him, her nails digging into his shirt as if to hold him there forever.

Part of him considered misting to another room or location, to escape this madness. But a more powerful part of him cried out in protest, telling him he wouldn't survive without this.

His mind spun, trying to sort fiction from truths, only to be distracted by Clara's mouth once more.

He'd stopped kissing her when he voiced her name.

Unacceptable.

His lips captured hers, vowing to never leave again.

He released her hair to ensnare both of her hips and lifted her up against him. Her athletic legs circled his waist, her hands sliding up to grip his shoulders.

It wasn't enough.

He needed them both naked. To be inside her. To *fuck* her.

His groin tightened with the prospect, his shaft impossibly hard. He'd always had to order his body to react. But not with Clara. For the first time in his life, his body commanded him.

He walked them into his bedroom, not bothering with the lights or to close the shades on the windows. The entire world could see this if they desired—a thought that intrigued him.

Would they envy him?

Desire the female wrapped around him like he was her sole reason for existing?

Mmm, an intriguing idea. He'd have to investigate that later, after he took off the edge a little. If that was even possible.

He laid her on his bed, his plush comforter framing the naked vixen in a sea of black. She gazed up at him with desire glistening in her blue eyes, her swollen lips engraved by the evidence of their kiss.

It was the most beautiful sight he'd ever seen. Even more stunning than all the colors of the council.

Clara didn't need wings to perfect her form. She was gorgeous without the feathers. He wanted to worship her with his tongue, to nibble every inch of her creamy skin. But his focus went to her breasts, to the rosy tips standing at attention and begging him for a kiss.

His blood heated with the thought, a foreign ache in his groin telling him to start there.

He pulled his shirt over his head and unbuttoned his pants to provide his throbbing arousal a little breathing room. Then he kicked off his shoes and crawled over her, his mouth skimming her supple flesh before settling over her erect nipple.

Clara sighed in response, her slender fingers weaving through his hair to hold him against her. He took that as a sign of approval and laved the tip to his heart's content before sinking his teeth into the curve of her breast.

She screamed in response, the sound one of rapture mingled with pain, and her body trembled violently below him.

An orgasm, he realized, his body tense with the thought.

He'd never seen a woman come undone like

this.

Sure, his previous encounters had experienced pleasure. But Clara resembled a goddess in the throes of passion, her expression glazed with the need for more.

He felt her dampening his pants, her splayed thighs cradling his hips.

What does she taste like? he wondered, the scent of her arousal sweet in the air. There was only one way to find out.

He kissed the bite mark on her breast and ventured downward, licking and nibbling along the way. Her grip tightened in his hair, her body bowing off the bed as he settled between her thighs.

"You smell edible," he whispered against her slick flesh, his mouth salivating for her. "I may never stop, Clara."

She vibrated in response, a cry parting her pretty lips as he slid his tongue along her delicate folds. *Fuck.* She tasted better than he imagined. With her blood still warm on his tongue, he indulged in the mix of flavors.

Sweet.

Tangy.

Addictive.

"Gabriel." The purr underlining his name caused him to stiffen even more in his jeans. He'd never realized how tight these pants were until now, the zipper pressing against him painfully. But he endured it for another long lick of her flesh.

So. Damn. Good.

She shuddered, her legs clamping down around him, encouraging him to continue. He found her clit and sucked it into his mouth, his gaze on her face, observing her reactions.

When he applied more pressure, her skin reddened with excitement, and her desire warmed the air. If he eased his suction, she shivered, causing a hint of torment to ripple through his borrowed empathetic ability.

Fascinating.

With each action, he elicited a new reaction. One he read with ease because of her essence mingling with his.

It was so much better than the colors and vividness of the Seraphim world.

Because he *enjoyed* doing this to her. Her pleasure increased his own, intensifying the moment and taking him to heights he'd never expected to experience.

Why had he avoided this all his life?

Why would Seraphim choose not to experience such a phenomenon?

He marveled at the complexity of it all, the mingling of electricity thriving through his bloodstream and the maelstrom curling inside his lower abdomen. His groin ached with the need for freedom, the pants cutting into him uncomfortably and forcing him to kick off his jeans.

His boxers remained, the cotton providing

enough give for him to continue indulging in the taste of Clara. She squirmed beneath his mouth, her body strung tight as she skirted the edge of another climax.

He took her swollen bud between his teeth and forced her to fall again, her scream a siren's song to his ears.

Little witch, he thought, captivated by the sight unfolding before him.

She writhed, her orgasm a masterful wave that threatened to take him under with her despite his cock being nowhere near her sweet warmth. He groaned, his craving for her mounting to a precipice that forced him to remove his boxers and palm his aching shaft.

He felt violent.

Crazed.

Furious at his loss of control.

And utterly lost to the demands of his body.

He needed a release. To come. To feel the slick sheath of her wetness coating his skin.

"Clara." He uttered her name like a plea, his gravelly tone one he'd never heard before. He didn't know how to move, how to breathe, how to do a damn thing other than stroke himself with harsh, fast movements.

Her hand touched his, her soft tones a hypnotic caress that calmed him. "I want you inside me, Gabriel."

Fuck, he wanted that, too. More than he wanted

anything else in his life.

All his responsibilities and vows fled his mind, replaced solely by the purpose of taking this female. He was consumed by it. Stolen. Destroyed. And reborn as a new man. One who thrived on passion and sex.

He couldn't remember why or how they'd gotten to this point, nor did he care to evaluate. All he desired was her. This. Fulfillment.

She spread her legs wider, her wet center an invitation he couldn't deny. He stroked himself once more, with her hand still on his, then knelt over her to position himself between her thighs.

Heaven kissed the throbbing head of his cock, the slippery opening a welcoming embrace that accepted him in a single thrust. A strangled sound escaped his throat, the gratification of sliding inside her robbing him of his ability to process.

He merely existed.

A being of lust.

Driven by immoral cravings and depraved desires.

A million ideas slammed through him all at once, each one dirtier than the last. He wanted to dominate this female. Fill her with his essence. Make her drink from him. Mark her very soul. And do it all again, over and over, until they were mindless creatures who were so full of sensation that they couldn't move.

He pumped into her, eliciting a sharp gasp from

her mouth.

More.

He pushed harder, and she responded by raking her nails down his arms.

Yes.

He palmed her cheek and kissed her while his opposite hand went to her hip to guide their movements. She slid her tongue into his mouth, taunting him into an intimate dance that he eagerly returned.

She moaned.

He groaned.

She cried out.

He growled.

It was a mixture of animalistic sounds that drove him onward, forcing his pace to speed up to a near-brutal one that she accepted without reserve.

Sweat slicked their skin, adding to the savagery of their coupling. They were entirely lost to each other and the empathy lingering between them. Gabriel reveled in it, allowed himself to feel every inch of his throbbing shaft as he pummeled her below.

His veins thrummed with vitality, causing him to shake in the impending oblivion. He wanted to feel it. Needed to experience the climax that awaited him. Longed to finally understand what he'd been missing all his life.

He felt it building, his lower abdomen igniting with a flame that singed his insides.

"Fuck," he breathed, his mouth against hers, their pants mingling as one.

Her lips skimmed his cheek to his ear. "Faster," she demanded.

The word stoked the fire within him, forcing him into action as her teeth grazed his neck. She sucked the skin there, drawing a groan from his throat. He wanted more of that, particularly around his cock.

No, he wanted to feel her lips everywhere. To watch her tongue lick a path along the edges of his abdomen all the way down to his groin. Then she would wrap her lips around him and suck him to completion, swallowing every drop.

The thought alone almost made him come. But some part of him wanted her to join him, to share in the oblivion of their fucking.

He slid his hand between them, his thumb finding her clit and applying the same sort of pressure that he had with his tongue before. She shook beneath him, her exhale hot against his throat.

He kissed her neck in kind, then licked the blood that remained against her skin. "Gabriel," she whispered. "I... I *need*..."

"Whatever you want, I'll give you," he promised, picking up his pace and reading her response through his new sense of empathy.

She was warmth personified, her aura a blanket of heat that kissed his skin and caused his muscles to flex to near pain. Fuck, he needed to explode, and soon. It was too much for him to hold in, the torrent of sensation whirling inside him and seeking release.

Her incisors pierced his skin, sending him over the cliff of oblivion with no hope of return. He'd never been bitten before. There was a reason for that, one he couldn't identify beneath the flood of sensation drowning him in an ocean of rapture.

Only, he was swimming alone, and that wasn't acceptable. He refused to suffocate on the sensations without her.

He returned her bite, forcing her to join him in the delirium, and a strange sort of connection snapped into place, shooting them both into the deep end beneath the euphoric surge of pleasurable insanity.

His essence emptied inside her as she squeezed him with her slick walls, draining him of his life and purpose and joining his spirit to hers.

He'd never felt so close to another person.

So… *bonded.*

His eyes flew open, his mouth releasing her neck. "Fuck!" He tried to release her, to pull himself out of her body, but the damage was already done, as evidenced by the blood on her mouth.

His sudden jolt away from her had caused her teeth to rip across his skin, but he couldn't feel the pain of her dislodged bite above the reality of what they'd just done.

A blood bond.

CHAPTER FOUR

GABRIEL

A. FUCKING. Blood. Bond.

The words roared in his thoughts, his body still spasming from their union below, his mind lost beneath a cacophony of sensations he couldn't fight or ignore.

He sensed her confusion. Her gratification. And her need for more.

A need that he echoed, his desire to fuck her again taking over his senses and making him pulsate inside her.

It was a violent spiral. A dangerous concoction. An enchantment he couldn't fight.

None of his warrior training had prepared him for this.

She'd charmed him with her blood, bewitching him into this emotional madness, and trapped him with a bite.

There was no going back.

Only forward.

Because killing her was no longer an option.

With his blood inside her, she would begin to transform into a Seraphim. His destined mate.

He could already envision her future, her back decorated with pale yellow feathers dipped in red. The yellow would rival her hair, while the red tinge would match his wings—a reflection of their bond.

He shuddered at the thought, his destiny warping in a second.

And still his dick pulsed, begging him to fuck, urging him to indulge his *mate* in the satisfaction they both craved.

He didn't love this female. But he did desire her. And the feeling was mutual.

Because with her blood, he maintained her empathy, perhaps indefinitely now.

Shit. This was bad. Not even a century of Seraphim reformation would save him now. Would they remove his wings as punishment? Would he even allow it?

"Gabriel?" Clara whispered.

It was then that he realized she'd gone completely still beneath him, her arousal a lingering scent that no longer overpowered her ability to think. He could *hear* her, the words of her mind littered with concern.

Because she could hear him, too. Had heard his thoughts about killing her, had seen his original intention of removing her should she prove useless to his plight. And rather than fix him, she'd just wrecked him.

He buried his face in her neck, uncertain of what to do next.

And she responded by wrapping her delicate arms around him. Holding him. Offering him comfort. A gesture no one had ever attempted in his presence before.

Mostly because they all knew better.

However, Clara was different.

She claimed to prefer actions over words, something she demonstrated now by continuing to hold him even while his mind rebelled against the embrace.

He wanted to throttle her.

Then fuck her.

Then throttle her again.

His body began to shake beneath the turmoil, his practical nature battling with his new affinity for emotions.

He felt lost. Broken. Annihilated by the most unsuspecting of beings.

A female with soft blonde ringlets and a face designed by the heavens.

He went to his elbows on either side of her head, staring down at her as she kept her arms around him.

No words.

Just a gaze.

Understanding shone in her pretty blue eyes. She knew they were connected. But she didn't appear all that fazed by it.

"You've bewitched me, little witch," he said, his voice gentle despite the accusation.

She shifted her hold, one of her dainty palms going to his cheek. "You saved me, guardian angel."

The statement was completely at odds with what he'd said, making him wonder if she'd heard him. Or perhaps they were just confessing things.

This woman had turned his world upside down, and he hated her for it. While also realizing it'd all been his own actions that had driven them toward this end.

He'd taken her blood first.

He'd misted back into her cell.

He'd agreed to bite her.

He'd then lost himself to the aftermath.

And now he could read from her aura that she hadn't realized what biting him back would do, yet she didn't regret it. She'd wanted to feed, to replenish her Ichorian spirit, and she'd more than fulfilled her quota.

With his blood inside her, she'd never be required to drink human blood again.

She lifted upward to kiss him, her lips soft against his. *It's going to be okay,* she seemed to be saying. *We'll figure this out.*

He was helpless to her actions, returning the embrace because it felt right, not because it made logical sense.

She'd demolished all his training. Reprogrammed his mind. Enchanted his soul.

"How are you not terrified?" he asked her, flabbergasted by her easy acceptance. "You've just bonded yourself to a warrior Seraphim. For eternity."

"There are worse fates," she whispered.

"You don't know that."

"I do," she replied.

"It's a loveless match," he said. "I'll never be capable of giving you anything more than lust."

She might have shattered his hold on emotions, but he was certain he couldn't learn to love. Particularly as they'd shackled themselves to each other in error.

She'd more likely grow to hate him than to love him as well. Not that they required such an emotion. It wasn't a mandate of the bond. But neither of them would be able to indulge another person sexually ever again.

Which meant he would become her lifeline for comfort.

And she would be the only one capable of making him experience ecstasy.

The latter didn't concern him. He'd gone decades without it. Surely, he could abstain again.

Only, his granitelike erection said otherwise. Because even now, in the seriousness of the emotion, he just wanted to thrust inside her and rut them both into oblivion once more. An entirely impractical notion, one he continued to consider despite his senses demanding otherwise.

She lifted her hips. "I'll accept lust."

"You're not thinking clearly."

"Neither are you," she returned, circling her legs around him and locking him deep inside her. "I don't want to think, just feel."

A statement that went against everything he was.

And one that sang to his newly fractured soul.

Because he could do exactly that—feel instead of think.

Tied to her, he could experience emotions and pleasure and forget the politics of the situation. Just for a moment.

It would be there in the morning when they woke.

He'd solve it then.

Yes, he liked this newfound resolve. This ability to merely exist without any repercussions. Oh, they would face them eventually. But for now, with her slick heat wrapped around his throbbing arousal, he preferred to indulge in the sensations over fretting about the outcome.

What's done is done, he thought.

Fuck me, Clara replied, her sultry tone forcing him to give her his undivided attention.

Okay, he agreed, moving inside her. *Hold on to me, little witch. I'm going to teach you how to fly.*

And he did, misting them up into the dark sky, to introduce her to their new life as bonded Seraphim.

She came apart in the clouds, her essence a drug he indulged in over and over again. Clara returned the favor in kind, introducing him to a whole new world of insatiability.

They continued well into the morning hours, not returning to his bed until they were replete and requiring rest.

Then he woke with his member in her mouth, and the whirlwind started all over again, the little witch overriding his sensible inclination.

It turned into a fuck-fest.

She took his decades of dissatisfaction and turned each experience on its proverbial head. Almost as though they were making up for lost time.

He memorized her with his mouth.

She licked every muscular line of his body.

They feasted on each other, living purely on sex and pleasure.

Until it was dark all over again. He finally forced them to pause, his stomach raging with a need for food—something he couldn't recall ever happening to him before. But they'd spent so much energy on one another that he'd depleted all his reserves.

"I thought Seraphim could endure almost anything," Clara murmured as he pulled on a pair of boxer shorts.

"I thought you didn't know anything about Seraphim."

"Just the myths, that you're impenetrable beings who probably don't exist."

He snorted, glancing back at her over his muscled shoulder. "Do I exist, Clara?"

Her blue eyes danced over his torso. "I think so, but maybe you should touch me again to confirm it."

"If I do that, we'll end up fucking. Again."

"And what a shame that would be," she drawled, stretching out like a succubus against his sheets.

"You're hungry, too," he reminded her, sensing her famished state.

"For you."

His lips nearly twitched. *I'm amused*, he realized, giving a shake of his head. *Why is this amusing?*

Food. He needed food. Then they could… do something.

Probably have sex again.

He preferred that over thinking about the ramifications of it all.

Reaching into his drawer, he grabbed a pair of boxer shorts and undershirt for her to wear. "I'm going to order something for delivery," he told her.

She accepted the clothes but set them beside her on the bed. "I can cook something."

"I have no food," he replied.

"Oh. If you have ingredients delivered, then I could cook something?"

He considered her. "What would you make?"

"Whatever you want."

"I typically eat protein and plant-based foods." He never really indulged in flavors. Given

55

everything else that had happened, he might as well consider changing that now. "Do you have a favorite meal?"

"I have several."

"Which one would you like to make?"

She bit her lip, considering. "Can I, um, surprise you?"

He blinked at her. "Why?"

"Because I want to," she replied, her cheeks flushing a pretty shade of pink. "Please?"

His gaze dropped to her mouth. "Will you suck my cock again later?"

The pink in her cheeks turned to a deep shade of red. "Yes."

He shrugged. "Then you can do whatever you want." He went into his office—which was technically a second bedroom—and found a tablet for her to use to order online. Then he brought it back to her in the bed. Her cheeks were still tinged with color. "Did I embarrass you with my directness?" he wondered out loud, trying to determine what the reaction meant.

She took the tablet from him. "Not exactly."

"Then why are you blushing?"

Her long blonde lashes fluttered as she gazed up at him. "Because now I want to suck on you as an appetizer."

His dick immediately hardened at the statement, shocking him into silence. His body *never* reacted like this. But just the mention of her sweet lips wrapped around his shaft had him groaning in discomfort.

She smiled before looking down at the screen. "I need you to unlock this."

He did what she wanted with a swipe of his finger, still unable to speak. Everything inside him hummed with anticipation of committing a dozen more sins with the still-naked female in his bed. She'd awoken a beast inside him that hungered for more.

And more.

And more.

Fuck.

He rubbed a hand over his face and left the room to search for his phone. What he needed was a practical distraction, something to remind him of his purpose in life.

Except the bond tugging at his insides pointed at his *new* purpose.

Stop, he commanded.

You don't want me to order? Clara replied into his mind, her soft tones far too welcome in his head.

I'm so fucked.

I don't understand.

I'm talking to myself.

Oh. She paused. *Uh, should I stop ordering?*

No, keep ordering. Let me know when you need a card for payment. He had all the information saved on his tablet, but it would require a password for her to use it.

She didn't reply, but her contentment radiated from the other room. Or maybe it was through their connection. He couldn't tell anymore because it was all fucking linked.

He cursed under his breath and focused on finding his phone, then remembered he'd left it in his jeans. Which were in the bedroom.

His eyes lifted heavenward before he could stop them. Rather than even attempt to rectify the misgivings on his face, he just misted to the other room to find his jeans.

Clara gasped when he arrived, her blue eyes wide.

"What?" he asked as he bent to retrieve his discarded pants.

"Your wings!" she exclaimed.

He arched a brow—another facial issue he chose to just ignore, but absolutely noticed—then he realized he was still in his ethereal state. "Oh. Right."

Had she not noticed those last night when he took her into the sky? Maybe it'd been too dark for her to see. With the clouds covering the moonlight, his color wouldn't have shown well. But they did now beneath the low lighting of the room.

She set the tablet down and moved toward him. He held his jeans between them like a shield, his hand gripping the phone in the pocket as she stopped before him. "Can I… touch them?"

He'd never been asked that.

It wasn't something a Seraphim would even think to do.

But as he'd broken pretty much every barrier with this woman, he didn't see the harm in allowing her to shatter another. "Yes."

CHAPTER FIVE

GABRIEL

CLARA's blue eyes glimmered with excitement as she reached out to stroke her finger along the edge of his red feathers. A warm emotion encircled her, the heat basking him in a strange sort of glow that heated his chest.

Happiness, he thought.

Pride, she corrected. *But it's often tied to happiness.*

"How do you know the difference?" he wondered out loud.

"Experience," she murmured, her fingers petting his wing now. "You'll learn." Her expression turned almost dreamy, stirring a lightness in the air.

"And what are you feeling now?"

"Content," she whispered. "But also safe." Her blue eyes met his. "Your wings are beautiful, Gabriel."

"You saw them last night."

"I was too lost to the sensations to notice. It's not every day an angel takes me into the clouds for a dozen orgasms." She dropped her touch, and his plumes flexed in response, irritated by the loss of her heat.

"You've destroyed me, little witch," he informed her.

"I'm not a witch."

"You are to me." He dropped his jeans but kept his phone in his palm. Then he used his opposite hand to grab the back of her neck and tug her to him. "Apparently, you're my little witch."

"Then you're my guardian angel."

She'd claimed that a few times. It didn't bother him. "My mother is from the messenger line, so I suppose it's appropriate."

"Messenger line?"

"Yes. I'm of the messenger and warrior lines."

"I don't know what that means," she admitted. It didn't surprise him, considering her lack of general knowledge about his kind. Their existence was a well-guarded secret, even against other immortals.

"I'll need to teach you about Seraphim politics," he decided out loud.

"Just as I'll need to teach you about emotions," she countered.

His lips nearly curled again, but he refused them. "A practical arrangement. I accept."

Her eyes sparkled. "I look forward to learning more."

"You might regret that statement once I start the

tutorial." Alas, understanding his world would be necessary for her survival.

Unless the council opted to exterminate her.

His brow furrowed with the thought. *Can they kill her?* he wondered. *Is she susceptible to death in this in-between state?*

Blood bonds were so rare that he wasn't sure.

Sethios and his mother weren't a good judge for developmental stages since both of them already possessed Seraphim genetics.

But Clara didn't.

Did that weaken her immortality?

The glimmer in her gaze died as she followed his thoughts. *Can who kill me?* she asked.

The High Council of Seraph.

Her face drained of color. *Why would they want to kill me?*

Because of our bond, he replied. *You're considered an abomination to my kind. Bonding with you is essentially a crime for Seraphim.*

Will they kill you, too?

I can't be killed, he replied. *But they may try to take my wings.* A punishment he'd recently learned existed for his kind. They'd done it to Skye and would likely consider doing it to him after everything he'd done these last few years.

Of course, they would have to catch him first.

Something he would not make easy for any of them.

Clara clutched his shirt. "I might die... because

of this?" A new emotion came from her, one he hadn't tasted yet.

Fear, he recognized, her eyes widening as her knuckles turned white.

"It's possible they will order your death, yes," he replied matter-of-factly.

She began to shake. He caught her with his arm as her knees buckled, his lips pulling down at the sight of her terror.

This wasn't a useful reaction.

Nor did he like it.

He guided her to the bed and helped her sit, then set his phone on the nightstand. "Clara?"

She was staring off into space now, her skin far too pale.

"Clara?" he tried again.

No reply.

She just sat there, fingers linked together, eyes on nothing. But her mind raced with thoughts, ones he snagged at different intervals as they tripped through her head.

Some of them were angry. Some were terrified. Some were resigned.

One lingered in regret, but she quickly dismissed it in favor of resignation. She chose the experience they shared over her own life, a fact that alarmed him because it made no logical sense.

"How can you think that?" he demanded. "We barely know each other. Your life is surely worth more than our bond."

"Is it?" she asked, her eyes still unfocused. "Do you know why I was turned?"

"No." He only knew Aidan had created her. He'd never looked into why, as it wasn't relevant.

"For Issac," she said. "Aidan turned me as a present for another man." She released a little laugh and shook her head. "He never asked me for permission. He just assumed I wanted immortality and handed me over like some glorified gift. The only reason I didn't hate him was because I could sense the reason behind it—the love."

Gabriel studied her. "Are you likening it to our situation of you turning into a Seraphim without permission?" he asked, unclear as to the reason for her story.

"No. I'm trying to explain why I find worth in the experience—because I more or less chose it."

That rationality didn't make sense. "You bit me without understanding the consequences."

"True, but I think I would do it again even if I did know."

His eyes widened. "You would choose to be bonded to a Seraphim you barely know?"

"If it means feeling a connection to someone for even five minutes of my life, then yes."

"I don't… I'm not sure I follow. Are you saying you don't have any connections?" Because that seemed illogical. Aidan created her. Did that not serve as a link in some capacity?

"How old are you, Gabriel?" she asked.

"Nearly six decades," he replied slowly, uncertain as to why she changed the subject but curious about her now as well. "You?"

"Ninety-three years old," she said. "My family died of the flu when I was seven. I was the sole survivor and grew up in an orphanage in Vancouver. So I learned how to be alone at a very young age. I was just nineteen when I met Aidan. He found me on the streets—a place a lot of girls in my situation ended up—and turned me a few days later."

"Which created a sire bond," Gabriel translated.

"Of a sort, yes. But you see, I've always had a gift for reading emotions. When I became an Ichorian, that talent grew into a supernatural ability. And so, I've always been in tune with the emotions of those around me. I could see their familial links, and not one of them connected back to me."

She described a rather lonely existence, but still, she had a link before him. "I'm sure Aidan cared for you in some way."

"Oh, he did," she replied. "But he never loved me. Neither did Anya or Nadia. Or Issac. Or Tristan. Or even B or Luc. We're family in a way, but not where it counts, something that became astutely obvious when they all so easily believed me to be the culprit. As I told you, actions are what matters to me. Not words."

"I don't love you," he said, feeling the need to

clarify that. "Our connection is by blood, not through the heart."

"I know."

"Yet you would still choose it?" He failed to understand her logic. "Why?"

"Because it's a connection I can feel," she said softly. "And I've always wondered what it would be like to experience that." Her smile was sad. "I don't expect you to understand, Gabriel. I know there's no love between us—I sense that, too—but I've been alone for so long that I'll accept pretty much anything at this point."

"That's very sad reasoning," he informed her. "You've not even lived for a century, and we just tied ourselves to one another for eternity."

"An eternity you just said might not happen because of your council." She picked up the tablet. "As I said, even if it's temporary, it was worth it to me to feel a semblance of belonging, despite it being done by accident." She held out the device for him. "Can you unlock this so I can finish my order?"

He swiped his finger across the screen. "You're not concerned at all about the council or your potential death?"

"Worrying about it will only waste precious life," she replied, her focus on the tablet as she continued her order. "And I learned long ago not to mourn situations I have no control over."

That... was actually rather practical.

The rest, however, baffled him.

She would prefer to link herself to him over living alone.

A bizarre decision, one he suspected she would regret once her shock wore off. Except he didn't sense any surprise from her, just a content warmth as she scrolled through the grocery list.

So maybe she was broken after all.

Or just severely damaged.

"If the council decides to punish us, I intend to fight," he told her.

"Okay."

"Will you fight as well or let them take you?"

She blinked her big blue eyes away from the screen to look at him. "Empathy isn't very useful in battle. It can only be used to determine someone's true intentions, to offer you a chance to act preemptively rather than reactively."

A fair assessment. But… "That doesn't answer my question."

"It does," she replied, returning to the tablet. "Empaths don't fight."

"So you'll let them take you?"

"I won't allow them to do anything, Gabriel." She typed something out on the screen and held it up for him. "Ready for payment."

He quickly processed it for her, then set the item on his nightstand beside his phone. "You will either fight or be taken."

"Or hide," she replied. "But as I said, I'm not worrying about something I can't change. When the future comes for me, I'll face it, and either survive, or not."

Another rational statement.

So maybe she wasn't broken, just... carefree?

Yet she'd been shocked at first. How had she gotten over it so quickly?

"By realizing there's nothing I can do to change it," she replied softly. "I'm not broken, Gabriel. I'm just trying not to worry about things I can't control. Is that really so hard to understand?"

"Yes," he replied. "Everything you've said in the last thirty minutes is difficult to process. I don't understand your reasoning."

"Not every decision requires logic. Some decisions are made from the heart." She pressed her palm to his chest. "Consider that lesson number one."

"Emotions don't play into Seraphim decisions," he countered. "Consider that your first lesson, too."

Her lips curled into an alluring grin. "Touché."

Rather than reply, he retrieved his phone again and noted the missed texts from Ezekiel and Vera. "Lizzie had the baby," he read to Clara. "And the council knows her location, but she's protected by wards." He expected as much. "Fortunately for us, that means they've directed the Fates to focus on Lizzie and not our bond."

A good indication that their new bond wasn't noticed. Or, if it was, it didn't take priority.

Ezekiel not mentioning it also suggested Skye hadn't seen it.

"Fates?" Clara repeated. "Also, thank you for the update on Lizzie. They're okay?"

"Yes, from what Ezekiel says, they're fine. And the Fates are a line of Seraphim who can see the future. The council uses them to guide their edicts. So if they haven't foreseen our bond, then it doesn't create any consequences worth noting. At least not yet. So the council likely hasn't been notified of it." He set his phone down again. "That's your second lesson."

She nodded, then shifted up onto her knees, her breasts swaying with the movement. Nudity clearly didn't faze her. And he really didn't mind that trait at all.

"Then I owe you a second lesson," she said.

His brow itched to lift, but he denied it. Again. "I'm listening."

Her eyes smiled, the enchantress coming out to play. "Actions, not words."

"Yes, I'm aware of that lesson already."

"No, I mean, I prefer to teach with actions"—she reached for his boxer shorts and tucked her finger into the band, yanking him toward the bed—"not words."

Oh. "Are you going to suck my cock now?" he asked.

"Lie down and find out."

Yeah, she didn't need to tell him twice. The

groceries wouldn't be here for another forty minutes, and they had nothing else to do. Well, other than go to Ezekiel's place. That was what the last message had demanded, but the others could wait for a bit.

Gratification over logic.

A new lesson, indeed.

CHAPTER SIX

CLARA

CLARA WATCHED Gabriel swallow his first bite of her beef stroganoff, but as usual, his expression gave nothing away.

However, she sensed his satisfaction through their link. Or rather, *bond*, as he'd called it.

She felt it anchored inside her, tying her to his existence. For whatever reason, that left her feeling safe and secure, not terrified or trapped.

Perhaps he was right about her being slightly broken. She'd endured a lot over her lifetime and had recently lost the only person she had a true connection to—her Sire.

Even though she and Aidan never loved each other, they had cared deeply for one another, similar to family. However, she'd always been last on his list.

Which was fine.

She was used to being last.

Except she'd never anticipated it blowing up the way it did with the Hydraians.

She shoved the pain away and focused on

Gabriel once more as he lifted his fork to his lips again.

He was shirtless at the table, clad only in a pair of boxers, his hair freshly damp from his recent shower. He'd taken one while she'd cooked. Then he'd misted out here, ready to eat, as soon as she had pulled the pan off the stove.

Her thighs still tingled from the two orgasms he'd given her after she'd gone down on him. It seemed her guardian angel liked oral sex.

She wondered how he'd feel about other activities... *like anal.*

He dropped his fork and looked at her. "Are we trying that next?"

"Is that lesson number three?" she countered.

He considered it, his face as serious as ever. "Yes." Then he resumed eating as though they hadn't just spoken about him taking her up the ass.

This man was a conundrum. Nothing fazed him, yet he'd expected her to react to the news of her potential death. Which, yeah, at first, it'd unsettled her. Just like the bond had. But once she resigned herself to having no control over it, she was fine.

And a tiny part of her trusted him to keep her safe. Not that she would voice that out loud. Mostly because she suspected he would deny it.

"This is satisfactory," he said after finishing over half his plate.

She smiled and started into her own dish, aware

that *satisfactory* was probably his version of a compliment. They'd work on that.

Well, they'd work on a lot of things. Now that they were bonded.

Warmth spread through her veins at the thought, the invisible anchor inside her grounding her in a way she'd never thought possible. She'd gone her entire life being everyone's second or third choice. And while she knew Gabriel would never love her, she felt his loyalty lingering in their connection.

He would never take another lover.

And neither would she.

Talk about a quick commitment, one that could pose a slight problem. "How will I feed?" she asked him after swallowing a savory bite of meat. "On blood, I mean."

"If you're craving it, you can have mine."

"Will that be enough to sustain me?" She felt rejuvenated and alive after imbibing some of his essence last night, but she wasn't sure how long that would last.

He stared at her for a moment, then a glimmer of understanding lit up his green eyes. "You no longer need human blood. Seraphim don't rely on the essence of others for survival. That's just a consequence of your resurrection."

He continued into a lesson on Osiris and how he'd created all of Ichorian and Hydraian kind through his blood as the Seraphim of Resurrection.

Clara had overheard some of this from the Elders after Stas's miraculous recovery, but she hadn't realized the full extent of it. No one ever really told her anything, she just gathered bits and pieces by listening to others speak. It was a result of her defenseless power. Or she thought that might be why she was often overlooked. Regardless, she appreciated Gabriel bringing her up to speed on the topic.

"So now that we're bonded, I'll become a full-blooded Seraphim," she said, already aware of that possibility from overhearing Gabriel's thoughts earlier. But saying it out loud somehow made it more believable.

"I believe so, yes. Issac—who has no Seraphim genetics inside him—has already shown signs of his ethereal growth. I imagine you will as well, starting with your waning need for human blood."

"Meaning you'll be the only source I need."

"You won't even need me," he replied. "But I don't mind you biting me again." His green eyes flickered with a subtle heat, just enough to thaw the colder features of his face and allow her a glimpse of the virile male beneath the stoic exterior.

She could also sense his growing interest at the prospect. If she looked down, she just might see that interest, too. But instead, she held his gaze and smiled. "I accept that invitation. And thank you for my lesson."

His lips actually twitched at her cheekiness.

Then he flattened them and worked on finishing his meal.

They ate in companionable silence until his phone began to chirp from the other room. He sighed and misted away from the table, his red feathers appearing in a gorgeous flurry before he blinked out of sight.

She caught one of the plumes he left behind and marveled at the soft texture. It reminded her of silk, yet electricity hummed along the edges.

He returned with the phone at his ear. "Yes" was all he said while a masculine tone conversed from the other line. She couldn't make out the words but recognized Ezekiel's deep drawl. "I had another engagement."

Her eyebrow winged upward at his flat tone.

"My schedule is my own," he said, his jaw clenching slightly with the words. Yet his voice remained toneless as he added, "I'll arrive when I feel like it." Then he ended the call and tossed the phone onto the table.

She set his feather down beside it, then gathered their plates. "I'll just clean this up."

He remained silent at her back while she washed their plates. But when she turned, she caught him staring at her ass. Her lips quirked up in response, and he gave her an unapologetic look.

"I would rather fuck you again than go to Iceland." His voice still lacked emotion, but his nostrils flared with the statement, and his aura radiated sexual intent. However, a hint of frustration rested beneath it all. The notion of sex before duty was bothering him.

"What's in Iceland?" she asked, assuming it was tied to Ezekiel somehow. He wasn't in the habit of spouting meaningless statements at her, so Iceland obviously held an importance.

"Ezekiel and Skye have a place there. They're expecting Lizzie and the others to arrive soon, and they need me to help ward the property for her protection."

Clara's eyebrows shot up. "Then why are you still here? That's more important than, uh, watching me clean up." Yeah, that wasn't what she meant at all, but she'd blushed enough during the last twenty-four hours.

Gabriel's directness was unlike anything she'd ever experienced. She liked the change of pace because he left nothing up to chance. He meant what he said—something his actions continued to prove.

"Will you come with me?" he asked.

She was surprised by the concern radiating off of him.

He palmed the back of his neck, grimacing a little. "I would also prefer you by my side, not in a Hydraian cell."

"I would prefer that, too," she admitted, her voice huskier than she intended. "What will we tell the others?"

"Nothing." He shrugged. "What's going on between us doesn't impact them."

"They're going to ask why I'm with you and not in Hydria."

"And I'll tell them I didn't care for your accommodations, so I removed you from the cell. If they have a problem with it, they can challenge me and lose." He sounded so confident in his assessment.

"Luc won't like it."

"Luc isn't my king," Gabriel returned. "Come with me."

Not a question this time, but a demand. One that had her lips curling. She liked bossy Gabriel. It gave him a sexy edge that added to his overall appeal. At least for her. A good thing, considering they were bound to each other forever now.

She'd never have sex with anyone else.

A strange realization, yet it didn't bother her. Her sense of empathy made it difficult to take others to bed anyway. She always had to ignore their underlying reasons for being there.

With Gabriel, it was pure lust.

She could handle that.

Just as she didn't mind going with him now. "I'll need something a little warmer for Iceland."

He nodded and disappeared in a whirl of red feathers. She giggled under her breath and returned to cleaning up the kitchen. He was still missing when she finished, so she busied herself with a much-needed shower and used the minimal products he had available. She found a comb in a drawer afterward to untangle her hair, then wrapped a towel around herself and sat on his bed.

Thirty minutes later, he finally reappeared with four shopping bags. He dropped them on the floor, his expression muddled with displeasure. "Women have too many sizes" was all he said before going into his own closet.

She bit her lip to keep from smiling at the disgruntled remark, then went through the clothing he'd apparently purchased for her.

Jeans.

Sweaters.

Boots.

Even a jacket.

But no underwear.

Either he'd done that on purpose, or he hadn't wanted to even try going through the lingerie area. Regardless, she made it work by putting on a pair of skinny jeans, boots that were only half a size too big, and a sweater that clung to her braless chest—the latter of which he noticed the second he walked out of the closet.

"That's distracting," he muttered.

"I have no bra," she returned.

He studied her breasts for a moment, then shrugged. "I'm okay with this distraction."

She laughed. "I bet you are."

"It will make disrobing you later easier, too. A practical notion."

"Very practical," she agreed.

He nodded, appeased by her acquiescence. "We'll go to Iceland now."

She ran her fingers through her damp hair and held out her hand. "I'm ready."

He misted to the other room first—probably to retrieve his phone—then appeared right in front of her with his chest against hers, smashing her hand between them. She blinked up at him in surprise, then gasped as his mouth captured hers in a long, sensual kiss. "You're very attractive, little witch," he whispered.

"As are you, guardian angel."

He pressed his forehead to hers. "I may need your help sorting through the emotions of others. I struggled in the store with all the humans around."

"The trick is focusing on one person's emotions and allowing it to override the others. I typically find the happiest one in the room and concentrate on their aura."

"Then I'll concentrate on you."

She frowned. "I'm not usually the happiest."

"I don't like happy," he replied. "But I... I find you sufficient."

"We're going to need to work on your compliments, Gabriel."

"I don't do compliments."

"Yes, that's becoming clear."

He nodded. "Good."

She just shook her head, amused by his bluntness. Her lips grazed his once more, then she wrapped her arms around him. "Let's go."

He returned her embrace, and his wings sprang to life around them, just before the world swirled in a kaleidoscope of colors. She closed her eyes, the dizziness nauseating her. Then the fresh scent of coffee tickled her nose.

"I assume this was your prior engagement?" Ezekiel drawled, his voice deep and holding a touch of knowledge.

Gabriel released her with a grunt, then disappeared, leaving her in the middle of a room with a couch and two chairs. The windows showcased a dark night with the moon radiating off mounds of snow.

Iceland, she thought. *Sounds right.*

"Hello, Clara," a soft voice chimed as a dark-haired female bounded down the stairs. "I'm Skye." Her bright blue eyes lacked a certain clarity, almost as though she wasn't really using them to see.

"Hi," Clara greeted, vaguely familiar with the woman. Something about her being able to see the future. But the last Clara was told, Osiris still had her in custody. That must have changed. Unless Gabriel had just left her in the middle of the lion's den.

Skye is free from his compulsion, her guardian angel

whispered into her mind. *Ezekiel is in love with her. She does not feel the same.*

Are you sure? Clara asked, noting the warmth surrounding Skye. *She's certainly giving off love vibes.*

You will explain that more when I return.

And where are you?

Creating runes.

Right. She had no idea what that meant but assumed it was tied to the wards he mentioned earlier.

"Aren't you supposed to be in a Hydraian prison cell?" Ezekiel asked as he slid his hands into the pockets of his trademark leather jacket.

"I didn't betray them to Osiris," Clara replied. "And Luc knows where I am." Or rather, he had when she was in New York City. She wasn't as sure about her current location.

"Gabriel," Ezekiel repeated, his lips curling. "You two seem rather comfortable together."

She took a note out of Gabriel's playbook and lifted a shoulder. "He took some of my blood to borrow my empathy."

"Oh?" Ezekiel arched a brow. "And what else has he borrowed?"

She shrugged again. "You'll have to ask him about that."

"Hmm." His gold-flecked black eyes danced over her. "I'll wait and see where this goes."

"See where what goes?" a familiar voice asked from the doorway as Balthazar stepped inside with a blonde at his side. His eyes widened upon seeing Clara in the living area. "What are you doing here?"

"Stark brought her," Ezekiel replied. "Then he disappeared to work on the wards. Or perhaps he had another *engagement*."

Clara ignored him and tried to empty her mind. Not that it worked. One look at B and she knew he could see right through. *Please don't.*

"Why did Stark bring her here?" he asked, his chocolate gaze on her, but the question was directed at Ezekiel.

"He didn't explain himself," the assassin drawled.

"He rarely does," the female beside B added.

Another Seraphim, Clara mused, noting the lack of emotions surrounding her. Yet somehow she oozed sex appeal with her thick blonde hair, pale skin, and pretty blue-green eyes. All she had to do was blink, and half the men in the world would kneel at her feet.

She looked at B, then back at the female, and then at B again. Talk about a dangerous pair. The sexual energy radiating off of them was potent and intoxicating.

Yet it didn't impact Clara at all.

Odd, considering her ability to sense such a thing.

Gabriel, she realized. *It's my link to Gabriel.*

Balthazar's eyebrows shot up, causing her own eyes to widen. *Oh, no. Please don't say anything.*

About what? Gabriel asked.

Not you. B. I'm pretty sure he knows, from reading either my mind or my emotions. She mentally shook her head and tried to talk to Balthazar again, begging him not to give her away.

He might not be able to hear you clearly, Gabriel informed her. *He can't understand Stas and Issac when they speak into each other's minds. But he'll definitely sense it.*

I thought he could hear everything?

You're bonded to a Seraphim now. Consider this a perk.

A perk? she repeated, mulling that over. *So he can't read my mind anymore?*

Sort of, he replied vaguely. *Just don't tell him anything. I expressed my irritation at Issac for bonding with Stas, and I'd rather not have my words thrown back at me.*

Wait, you're against bonds? She wasn't sure how she felt about that.

They're sacred and tie the two beings for eternity. It's a rather large commitment.

Um, but you seemed okay with our bond. His actions had suggested his acceptance, too. Unless he'd changed his mind since?

I am okay with it, Clara. That doesn't mean the others will be.

His words mildly placated her, only to be disrupted by B clearing his throat. "Does Luc know you're here?"

"Gabriel said he's aware, yes." *Did you tell Luc I'm in Iceland with you?*

No, Gabriel confirmed. *Ezekiel will inform him if he deems it important. I assume he also told him you were in New York City.*

I thought you told Luc?

I told Ezekiel, he corrected. *He passed along the message to Luc, just as he sent Luc's response back to me.*

Which said?

In summary, he didn't approve, Gabriel replied flatly.

You failed to mention that.

As I don't answer to him, I didn't feel it was relevant.

She sighed. *Okay, but I don't want to anger him.*

It's not you he was angry with, little witch, he assured her. *And I'm not afraid of the Hydraian King. You're my bonded mate now. He can't touch you.*

She shivered at the possession in his tone, then froze beneath Balthazar's narrowed gaze. *Yeah, B definitely knows.*

It's not his business to share, Gabriel replied, his tone suggesting a lack of concern. *And if he does, we'll ignore them all. This is between us, Clara. Only us.*

Okay, she whispered back to him. *Only us.*

The female shared a look with B, then said, "I'm going to go check with Gabriel about the wards, then head back for Jay and Liz." A cloud of stunning purple feathers appeared around her, causing Clara's eyes to widen even more.

Oh, wow, she has beautiful wings.

So will you one day, Clara, Gabriel replied softly. *I look forward to seeing them in my bed.*

Her cheeks heated at the intimacy of those words. *Shouldn't you be focusing on the wards?*

I excel at multitasking. The arrogance in his mental voice was very him.

Yes. You do, she agreed.

"What else was Luc told?" B asked, drawing her back to him and his knowing gaze.

"Uh." She cleared her throat. "I, um, don't know."

"I see." B pulled out his phone and dialed, his eyes holding hers the entire time. "Have you heard from Stark lately?" He waited, listening as the Hydraian King—or she assumed that was who he'd called—responded. "So Mateo saw it." Balthazar nodded at whatever Luc said in reply. "Are you on your way here?" The deep baritone rumbled over the line, causing B to nod once more. "See you soon."

He hung up, his eyes still glued to Clara.

Then he shifted his focus to Ezekiel and Skye. "We need to talk."

She took that to mean she was off the hook. For now, anyway.

"We always need to talk," Ezekiel drawled, collapsing onto the couch. Skye settled beside him, her blue eyes still unfocused.

"Osiris," B replied. "Specifically, his history with the council. And what his intentions are now."

"You assume I know?" Ezekiel asked, arching a black brow into his equally dark hairline.

"I know you do." B folded his arms. "Start talking."

Ezekiel merely smiled. "Well, once upon a time..."

The Immortal Curse Series Continues with
Wicked Bonds

Curious about how Ezekiel met Skye? Find out in Blood Skye, *an Immortal Curse world novella.*

Craving more Immortal Curse fun? Check out Elder Bonds *for some stories from B and Luc, including the introduction to how B met Leela. Or start the Immortal Curse series with* Blood Laws.

Looking for more angels? Hang out with Eve in Daughter of Death. *She's been accused of a murder she didn't commit and has to work with her sadistic ex to prove her innocence. Just another day in paradise... or hell.*

Until next time. xx

Continue the Immortal Curse journey with Balthazar and Leela in Wicked Bonds...

Welcome to the Immortal Curse world where angels and vampires exist in secret... for now.

A passionate affair of sizzling heat.
Forgotten and buried.
Because what happens in Brazil stays in Brazil.

That was the plan, anyway. Until Balthazar started to remember everything. Now he's forcing Leela to pay the ultimate price—by making her *beg*.

Every hot touch ignites her soul. Every smoldering

glance makes her thighs clench. And worse, there's no escaping him.

They're on the run from a horde of warrior angels, protecting an innocent from a fate worse than death.

The High Council of Seraph has issued an edict.
Comply or die.
Only the faithful will survive.

WICKED BONDS

BLOOD SKYE
AN IMMORTAL CURSE WORLD NOVELLA

*In a world of cursed immortal beings, a seer is on the run
from a master assassin and his wicked bite.*

Skye craves freedom. Her wings. The ability to just
breathe.
Only, every destiny results in more chains.
Whether it be a slave to the High Council of
Seraph, or the plaything of the dangerous assassin
who hunts her, she's forever a prisoner.

It's the fate for all of her kind—always coveted for
their foresight.
Skye can predict all the various paths and outcomes
and knows how to weave her way between them.

Which is why she's on the run, even though she
knows how her destiny ends.
In *his* arms.
The dark assassin of her nightmares.

Gold-flecked black eyes.
Long, ebony hair.
A sinister smile.
And a soul as cold as ice.

She sees him everywhere. Even in her fantasies.
But she'll never let him win.
Not even when he catches her.

*You can lurk in the shadows all you want, dark angel of the
night. I'll never give you my heart. Not even when you beg.*

Blood Seeker

Seraphim do not feel.
Seraphim do not love.
Seraphim do not react.

Those are the rules every higher being lives by.
And Caro broke them all for *him*.

Now she's lost in a vacant sea, punished for the
ultimate sin of choosing an abomination—*a vampire*
—over her duty.

Sethios promised to come for her, to find her, to save
her, but with each passing breath, her hope melts
into despair.

Will he find her in time? Or will her mind shatter
from the madness?

Welcome to the Immortal Curse world.
The High Council of Seraph will see you now...

USA Today Bestselling Author Lexi C. Foss is a writer lost in the IT world. She lives in Atlanta, Georgia, with her husband and their furry children. When not writing, she's busy crossing items off her travel bucket list. Many of the places she's visited can be seen in her writing, including the mythical world of Hydria, which is based on Hydra in the Greek islands. She's quirky, consumes way too much coffee, and loves to swim.

Want access to the most up-to-date information for all of Lexi's books? Sign-up for her newsletter.

Lexi also likes to hang out with readers on Facebook in her exclusive readers group - Foss's Night Owls.

Oh, and don't forget to check out B's Blog for exclusive Hydria updates (if you're into that kind of thing).

Where To Find Lexi:
www.LexiCFoss.com

Blood Alliance Series - Dystopian Paranormal

Chastely Bitten

Royally Bitten

Regally Bitten

Rebel Bitten

Kingly Bitten

Dark Provenance Series - Paranormal Romance

Heiress of Bael (FREE!)

Daughter of Death

Son of Chaos

Paramour of Sin

Elemental Fae Academy - Reverse Harem

Book One

Book Two

Book Three

Elemental Fae Holiday

Immortal Curse Series - Paranormal Romance

Book One: Blood Laws

The Beginning

First Offense

Royal Fae Wars - Omegaverse Paranormal

Wicked Games

Underworld Royals Series - Dark Paranormal Romance

Happily Ever Crowned

Happily Ever Bitten

X-Clan Series - Dystopian Paranormal

Andorra Sector

X-Clan: The Experiment

Winter's Arrow

Bariloche Sector

Other Books

Scarlet Mark - Standalone Romantic Suspense